# The Sunset Pond

Written by Laura Appleton-Smith

Illustrated by Jonathan Bumas

**Laura Appleton Smith** was raised in Vermont and holds a degree in English from Middlebury College. Laura is a primary schoolteacher who has combined her talents in creative writing and her experience in early childhood education to create *Books to Remember*. Laura lives in New Hampshire with her family and her dog, Jake, who is featured in this book as Bud.

**Jonathan Bumas** attended Pratt Institute, The University of New Mexico, and Princeton University, which awarded his novella, *Toward the Gardens*, the Samuel Shellabarger prize. He has illustrated *Phonethics*, by John Ciardi, and *Poison Pen*, by George Garrett, as well as many book jackets. His work is reproduced in *The Art of Pastel Portraiture* (Watson-Guptill, 1996) and is represented by the Mulligan-Shanoski Gallery.

## A Book to Remember™

Published by Flyleaf Publishing
Post Office Box 185, Lyme, NH 03768

For orders or information, contact us at **(800) 449-7006**.
Please visit our website at **www.flyleafpublishing.com**

First Edition
Library of Congress Catalog Card Number: 97-61171
ISBN 0-9658246-8-3 PB
ISBN 0-9658246-3-2 HC

*Many thanks to the children in my classroom who have helped me to understand the deep value of the early reading experience.*

*And to Terry–without your support, this book would not be.*

*LAS*

*For Martha.*

*JB*

It is half past six and the sun has just begun to set in the west.

Matt asks his mom and dad if he may run with Bud to the Sunset Pond.

Mom and Dad tell Matt,
"Yes, but plan to be back at dusk."

Matt and Bud jump from the front steps
onto the soft grass.

They run past the beds of daffodils
and down the hill to the Sunset Pond.

Matt picks up a stick and tosses it in the pond for Bud.

"Jump in, Bud," yells Matt.

Bud jumps in the pond and swims fast to get the stick.

He huffs and puffs as he grasps it
and swims back to Matt.

Bud drops the stick in front of Matt.

Matt pats him and tells him that he is the best dog.

Bud wags big wet drips on Matt's legs and hands.

Just then Bud stops and scans the pond.

"What is it, Bud?" asks Matt.

In the pond is a log and on the log is a big bull frog.

Bud jumps back in the pond and swims to the frog as fast as he can.

"Jump, frog, jump!" yells Matt.

Bud swims fast, but just as he gets to the log
the frog hops off and lands with a "plop" in the pond.

The frog is quick to swim into a clump of grass on the bank of the pond.

In the grass, the frog is hidden and Bud cannot spot him.

Bud swims back and sits next to Matt on the dock.

Bud naps as Matt skips rocks on the pond.

As the sun slips past the hills in the west,
the pond glints red and pink.

A duck lands on the pond and drifts in the sunset.

The pond is still.

When it is dusk, Mom claps her hands
and Matt and Bud run back up the hill.

Matt stops and picks a daffodil for Mom.

For Matt and Bud, the pond is the best spot
to visit at sunset.